Pig and Penguin's
Party Planning Problems

Written and Illustrated
By

Erik Niel

First Edition.

To my wife, Jacqui, who believed in this story, to my family and friends who helped
me to see the dream through to a finished product, and to those who have
encouraged and supported the development of this book, I thank you...

ISBN - 978-0692477069

www.erikniel.com

For
Sophia and Grace,
The inspiration behind this story...

Pig and Penguin's

Party Planning Problems

Written & Illustrated
By

Erik Niel

Pig and Penguin met at the park across from their houses on Pennrose Place. The point of their meeting was to plan a party, and of course to share their favorite snack of peanut butter on pumpernickel. "I propose a proper luncheon," suggested Pig, "complete with pleasantly presented platters of fresh picked produce and pitchers of refreshing punch."

"Prestigious art will be displayed," continued Pig, "with paintings and pictures of people, palaces, petunias, or whatever leads one to ponder; producing interesting conversation amongst our peers. A posh party will be positively perfect."

Penguin frowned promptly. "It seems to me, that people will be more likely to be present if the party had a theme of say...pirates! We could have pirates with eye-patches, pesky parrots, popular party-food like pizza and popcorn, and plenty of playful pranks!" Penguin propelled himself to his feet and acted as if pointing a sword at Pig. "Say, we might even design a pirate ship to playfully push our guests off the plank!"

   Much to Penguin's surprise, Pig was not pleased with his pirate party idea. Pig plopped to the ground and sighed plainly. "Our proposals are very opposite. How can we possibly pull off such a party to please all of our pals?" Penguin persisted with the pirate party plan, promising that every person invited would be pleased at the playful plot. But Pig was not in positive agreement and pompously defended his position. "Proper and posh is perfect for my peers," proclaimed Pig, "and if no pact for planning can be in place, then I will present my own private party, without pirates!"

   "Pish posh," sneered Penguin. "I will plan MY own party, with positively no properness, only pirates and playful pirate behavior!"

So Pig and Penguin parted ways; each of them preparing separate party plans without procrastination. Pig began his planning by printing professionally designed invitations on pearl colored paper and placed them in periwinkle envelopes. He then proceeded to hand-deliver his invitations to his peers personally, and explained the premise of the perfectly proper luncheon.

Penguin also began to prepare by creating posters of treasure maps with precise details and directions to his party. He proudly posted them around town with hopes that his pals would be present. He also opened the pirate party invitation to the town's entire population, inviting as many guests as possible.

However, Pig did not invite Penguin.

And Penguin did not invite Pig.

With both parties planned for noon on Thursday of the same week, Pig and Penguin progressed with preparing for their events. Pig purchased exotic produce, more pumpernickel for petit sandwiches and pistachio pudding to put in his perfectly polished parfaits.

The pirate party at Penguin's place began to pull together too. Penguin transformed his patio into the deck of a pirate ship. On the portside, he put a plank that stretched out over the pool. Penguin also put up full-sized plastic palm trees and placed a few pesky parrots around the ship for his guests to peruse.

Pig noticed that the party Penguin was planning was to be held outdoors. "I'll not subject my peers to such painful noise and pre-school child's play. I'll proceed with hosting my guests indoors in the parlor." Pig's party planning was precise and perfectly presented. In addition to his prestigious dining program, Pig hired an ensemble of musicians to play classical pieces for entertainment. The combined performance of the piccolo, pan flute, piano, and light percussion would surely be pleasing to the party's atmosphere.

Penguin put on his eye patch and practiced his pirate impersonation. "Arrrrrgh," he snarled proudly at his reflection. "I'm positive that this pirate party will be perfect!"

The day of the parties arrived.

Pig peered out of his window, looking toward Penguin's house. He admired the pirate ship patio, the palm trees, and all of penguin's other preparations. "What a pity," Pig pondered, feeling poorly for being prideful against his friend. Pig was sad that he wouldn't get to see Penguin's party.

Pig thought so much of his problem with Penguin, that he lost track of time. "My guests will be present soon. I must be prompt in completing my preparations!" In a panic, Pig quickly positioned his serving platters in the parlor and stirred the pineapple punch. As promised, his party began precisely at noon with the arrival of his punctual peers, Porcupine and Platypus. The piano ensemble began to play as the other guests arrived.

Next door, Penguin's pirate party progressed into a playful extravaganza of fun. Penguin's pals Panda and Pelican put on their eye-patches and playfully pressured the other guests to 'walk the plank' into the pool below. At Penguin's party, there was plenty of pizza, pretzels, peanuts, potato chips, and soda pop, as promised, for his friends. The guests of the party were very pleased. Puffin perked up a proud statement to Penguin saying, "This is positively the best party ever!" Penguin smiled, and encouraged his pirate crew to begin the swashbuckling with a food fight. "In pirate fashion," Penguin proclaimed, "we must portray the characters for which we are pretending to be. Would a pirate eat this meal properly? NO!"

"Arrrrrgh!" shouted his mates, complimenting his proposition. At that instant, Panda picked up a handful of popcorn and threw it at Pelican. The guests paused for a moment, and then purposefully tossed anything they could get their paws or feathers on to whoever was in their closest proximity. Penguin playfully threw pretzels at Pony, who then tossed peanuts at Polar Bear. In searching for something to project in return, Polar Bear found a big bowl of plum pudding to which he added pickles, pears, pasta and pistachios to launch at precisely the right moment. Soon all of his pals were in a party food battle, and Penguin was pleased.

Inside the parlor at Pig's house, the posh and proper party was progressing smoothly. Pig's guests were impressed with the appetizers and musical accompaniment. "How delightful," stated Peacock. "Yes," added Poodle, "Your papaya and pomegranate pie is perfection. This is quite possibly the best party ever!" Pig blushed proudly, and bowed politely to accept his applause.

Just then, Pig's moment of pride was interrupted as a piece of pizza plopped firmly against the parlor's window. All of his guests paused, as Pig paced angrily to the window to see Penguin's party completely out of control. Pig raised the parlor window and called to his friend, "Penguin. Oh, Penguin!" But Penguin could not hear Pig over the powerful blast of noise and music at the pirate party.

Pig excused himself properly from his peers and proceeded outside to peek over the pinewood fence that separated him from his neighbor. "Penguin, Penguin," he pleaded. "Please have your pirate party patrons calm down. Your food fight has produced a piece of pizza planted on my parlor window!"

Startled by Pig's petition, Penguin turned to address Pig but instead slipped on a pickle and fell back into Panda. Panda then bumped into Pony, who upon pushing forward landed forcibly onto the end of the party food table where sat Polar Bear's plum pudding projectile prank. The bowl of pudding catapulted straight toward the open window of Pig's parlor room. Pig, Penguin and the pirate guests watched as the pickle, pear, pasta and plum pudding, propelled through the window and crashed into the center of Pig's Party covering his guests in the messiest of pirate pranks.

Pig panicked. All of his hard work to present a proper, posh party for his peers had now become a plum pudding disaster. Poodle, Platypus, Peacock and Porcupine, now covered in a purple sticky goo, pushed impatiently out of Pig's backdoor and paraded toward the Pirate party. Pig joined the procession and pressed harshly against Penguin's gate to enter onto his patio. Penguin and his pals were slightly fearful of the displeasure of Pig and the others. "Penguin!" Pig shouted as the posh party guests plowed toward the pirates, ready to engage in a return battle. "Arrrrgh!" cried the pirates as they powerfully projected the party food at Pig's angry peers. Porcupine pitched pineapple at Pony, as Pelican pelted Poodle with peanuts. Panda pegged platypus with pistachios and Puffin plastered all of the guests with a shower of pineapple, soda pop punch. A full out projectile war of potato chips, pasta, pizza, peas, pancakes, pepperoni, parmesan, and peppermints continued between both parties.

"Penguin!" called Pig as he noticed that his friend was about to be pummeled by a sweet potato pie. Pig pushed Penguin out of the harmful path, and found himself coated by the pie instead. All of the guests halted their projections and turned toward Pig and Penguin. "Thank you, Pig," said Penguin, proud of his friend for protecting him despite their party planning disagreement. "I'm sorry I was prideful about planning my pirate party, and not partial to your suggestions. Can you forgive me, Pig?"

"Of course, Penguin, but can you forgive me?" Penguin paused a moment, and then paced the patio deck. Both parties were surprised that Penguin had not immediately accepted.

"Yes, Pig, I too will accept your apology, but only pending one primary request."

"Anything, Penguin," pleaded Pig. "Anything!"

Penguin peered intensely at his friend, and as a great leader of pirates, he pronounced in a snarly tone, "Walk the plank!" Pig and Penguin's guests cheered as Pig playfully paced slowly toward the portside. Penguin followed close behind, ensuring his friend would partake in his peace offering. Pig proceeded to the end of the plank and pivoted to face his peers. "Thank you, Penguin," he stated with a smile. "I have very much enjoyed your party." Pig jumped into the pool below. All of the guests cheered as the parties resumed, with cheers to both Pig and Penguin for having quite possibly, no positively, the best parties ever.

The End.

For more information about
Erik Niel
Please visit <u>www.erikniel.com</u>

Made in the USA
San Bernardino, CA
30 March 2017